MiMi & Boppie

Pacifiers Thrown Into An Unexpected Situation

Written by Aminata Solammon

Illustrated by Janelle Dingle

To the Heath Family

ISBN: 5707304

ISBN-13: 978-1517111465

Leilah & Elijah, you are my inspiration.
Your creativity is amazing.
My love for you is never ending.

Daniel, thank you for supporting all
of my dreams and desires. I love you.

L.E.A.D

"Wheeeee!", MiMi said as she soared through the air.

Whizzing past the nursery door she noticed the shiny door knob.

As MiMi bounced across the wood floor she saw tiny bread crumbs and colorful snack wrappers.

MiMi looked up, down, and around. "I'm in the kitchen", she said with confidence.

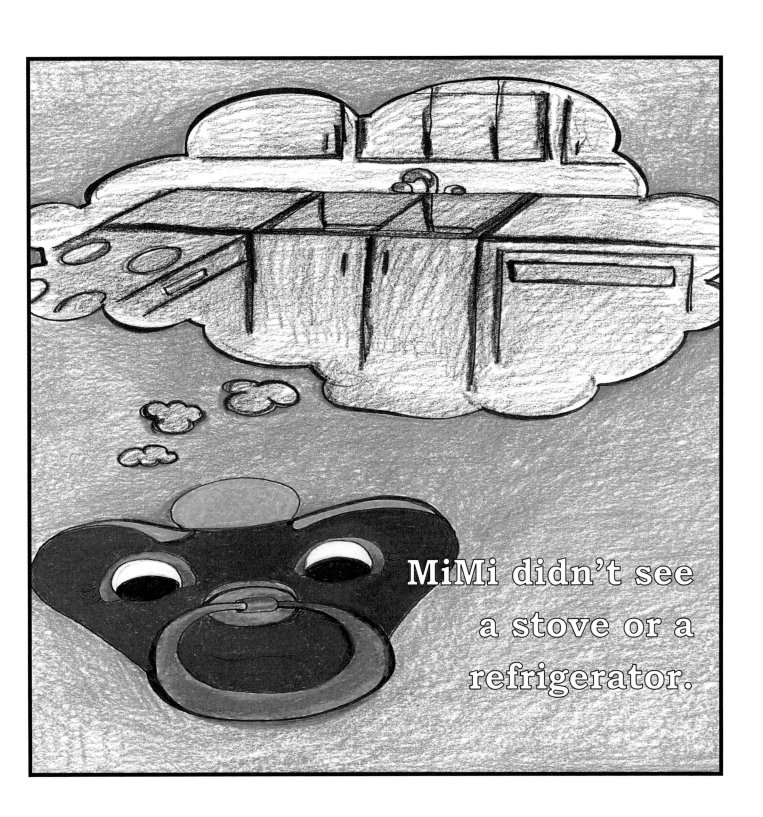

MiMi didn't see a stove or a refrigerator.

She looked up, down, and around. MiMi saw shiny dimes, nickels, and pennies everywhere. She was certain of her location this time. Mommy's purse!

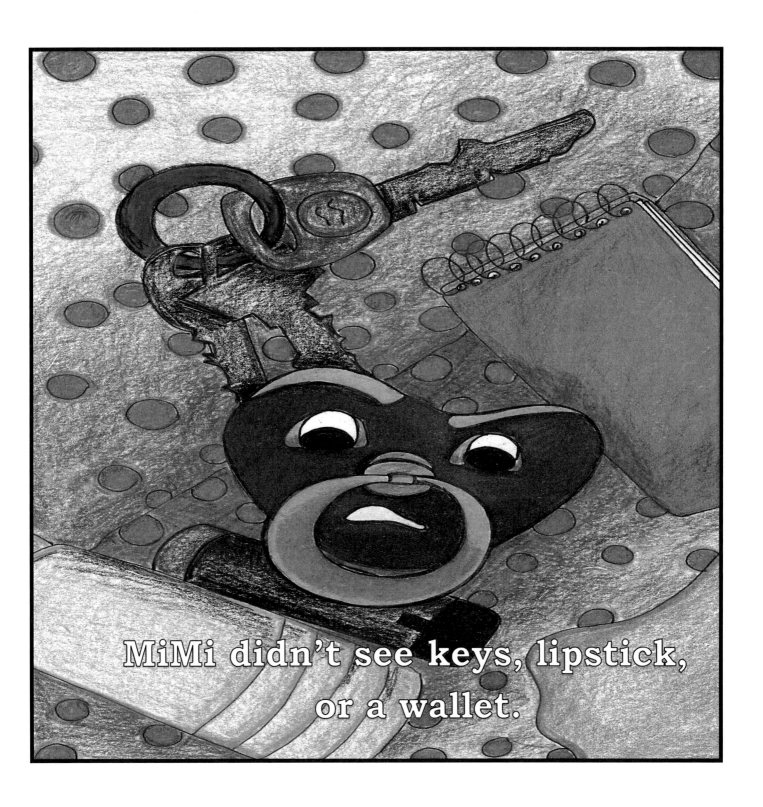

MiMi didn't see keys, lipstick, or a wallet.

She tried to stay calm, but MiMi was a little nervous. She'd never been in this part of the house before.

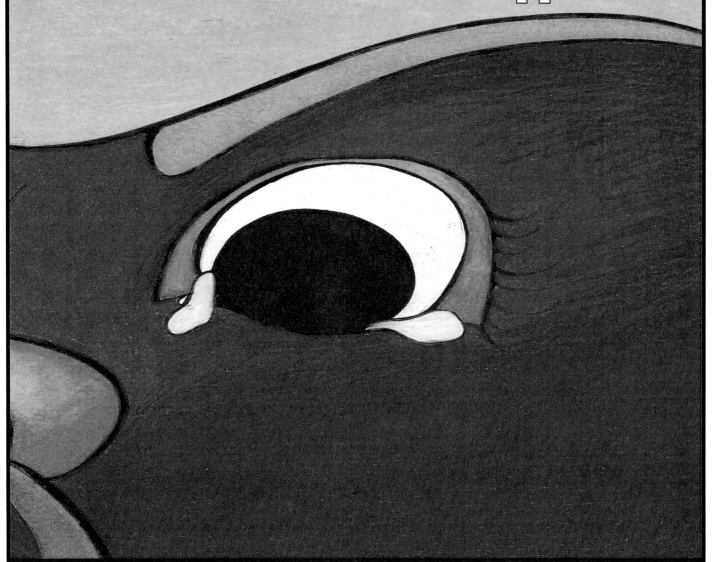

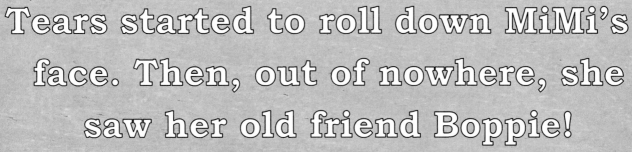
Tears started to roll down MiMi's face. Then, out of nowhere, she saw her old friend Boppie!

"Where have you been?", she asked. Boppie began to talk nonstop. "Well, I've been here since breakfast", he told MiMi.

"I thought we could all be friends", he said. "But whenever Sippy Cup was around Baby would snatch me out of his mouth and fling me across the room."

"This game went on for weeks."

"We even played in the car", Boppie said laughing a little.

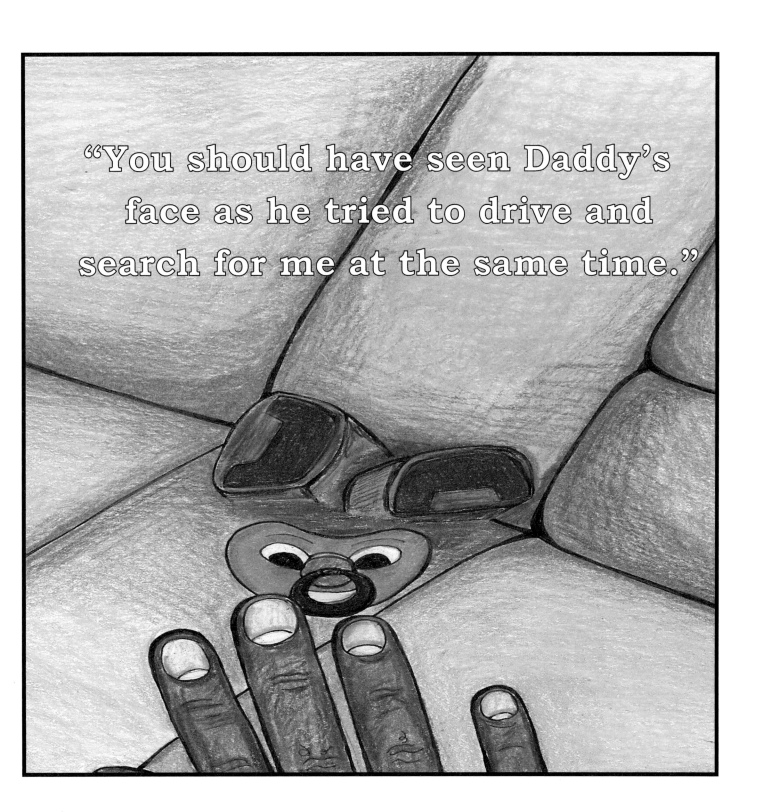

"The last time Baby and I played the game was at breakfast. Baby wouldn't stop crying", Boppie explained.

"I landed here with the bread crumbs, snack wrappers, and shiny coins", Boppie told MiMi.

MiMi looked up, down, and around. Tears started to roll down her face. She moved closer to Boppie and asked, "Exactly, where are we?"

Boppie looked up, down, and around. He moved closer to MiMi and slowly replied, "I don't know."

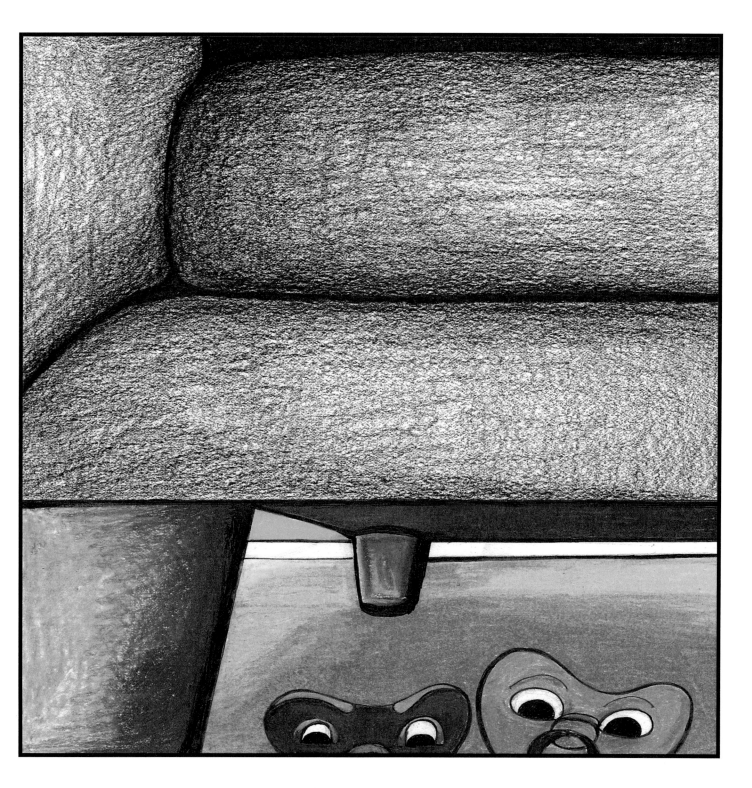

THE END

MiMi & Boppie was inspired by the author's children, Elijah and Leilah.

One day Elijah couldn't find his favorite pacifier and began screaming for "Boppie". His parents finally figured out that he wanted his pacifier.

Imagine how surprised they were when several years later, their daughter, Leilah began screaming for "MiMi". They quickly realized she too, had given her pacifier a name.

Both Mimi and Boppie were notorious for getting lost everywhere, including the kitchen, the living room, and the car.

Elijah & Leilah

A wife and mother of two, Aminata Solammon is an Atlanta, GA native and owner of Artivity Zone, an arts crafts party entertainment company.

The company's mission is to combine arts & crafts to create fun and educational activities for children of all ages. Artivity Zone's activities support developmental skills including: sensory-motor, cognitive, emotional, and social.

In addition to parties, Artivity Zone connects with the community and hosts story time & crafts at local libraries and schools.

To round off her time, Aminata enjoys writing and is excited about her next book _LuLu the TuTu._ A story about a tutu who loses her colors and has to reconnect with nature in order to find them.

Made in the USA
San Bernardino, CA
28 April 2017